# Return to the Most Beautiful Village in the World

**Yutaka Kobayashi**

Museyon, New York

Since he left his small village in Afghanistan,

Mirado has been traveling around the world with the circus.

He has gotten used to living in strange places.

But every day, he remembers the village of Paghman and his friend Yamo.

"I wonder how Yamo is doing."

Another winter has come.

On the radio Mirado hears the news that the long war is coming to an end.

Mirado remembers the song that his father sang to him when he was small.

♫ *DARA BA DARA*

*From valley to valley*

*I send a wind of Paghman to you.*

*It travels over green wheat fields,*

*It blows your hair,*

*From afar, from me.* ♫

Mirado, the flute player, is everyone's favorite in the circus.
Wherever he plays, whenever he plays, people soon gather.
"Encore!" "Encore, Mirado!"

But something is bothering Mirado.
The flute that he has traveled with has started to crack.
The flute is precious to him because it was given to him by his father, who
went to war and has still not come back.
Even so, Mirado plays beautifully.
"The circus will soon begin!"

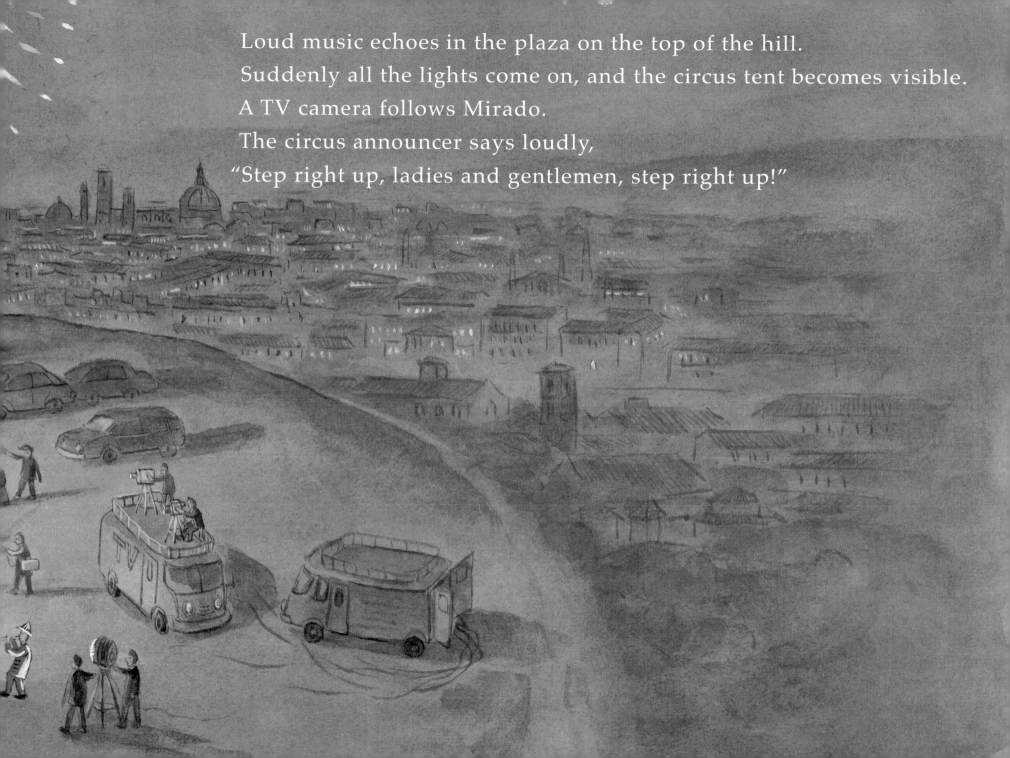

Loud music echoes in the plaza on the top of the hill.
Suddenly all the lights come on, and the circus tent becomes visible.
A TV camera follows Mirado.
The circus announcer says loudly,
"Step right up, ladies and gentlemen, step right up!"

The circus has begun.

When Mirado appears on the stage, the tent becomes very quiet.

He plays many different kinds of songs.

At the very end he plays the song his father taught him. He plays with all his heart.

♫ *DARA BA DARA*

*From mountain to mountain,*

*I send a wind of Paghman to you.*

*It travels through golden fields,*

*It brings love to you,*

*From afar, from me,*

*who cannot see you.* ♫

The circus arrives in the next town.

Mirado has been thinking about something for a long time. Now he tells the circus master.

"I would like to go back to Paghman."

The circus master looks out over the ocean and nods.
"If that is what you want." He doesn't say anything else.

The farewell party for Mirado lasts late into the night.
The circus master takes off his scarf and wraps it around Mirado's neck.
Mirado buys seeds for a lot of crops in the town
and packs them inside his luggage.

Then he carefully packs his father's flute, which has finally stopped making sound.

Early next morning, Mirado boards an eastbound train.
His black bag is filled with souvenirs for Yamo.
He is excited at the thought of seeing his friend again.

Mirado transfers from the train to a bus and gets off at the last stop.
There is nothing else to do but to walk after this point.

"I can give you a ride on this for a while,"
a kind man says to Mirado.

When he gets off the wagon, he is all alone.

Mirado walks. He passes by villages,
through forests, and over hills.
It's winter, so there is no one living in the huts
in the highlands.

He crosses many borders and still he walks.
When he thinks of Yamo, his feet just keep
moving forward.

He passes through a town in the middle of a plain.
From there the path leads into the mountains.

A girl who is taking care of some cows gives Mirado fresh milk.

Before sunset, he sees a shepherd boy coming down from the mountains. "It is going to be dangerous after this," the boy tells Mirado. "There are soldiers and mountain thieves and wolves. The wolves will come out when it gets dark."
The boy gives his staff to Mirado. "Please take care."

When the sun sets, it gets cold.

Mirado feels tired and lonely.

He is very hungry too. He sees the light of a bonfire in the distance.

"What if those people are dangerous?"

The man waves at Mirado.

"You must be cold. Come here and warm yourself by the fire."

"You must be hungry. Have some bread and soup," the woman says to him.

Mirado is relieved and sits down.

"Where are you heading?" Mirado asks. "We're on our way back to our village. We lost everything in the war. We're going to cultivate the fields and start all over again." The moon rises in the sky. The man takes out a flute.

He starts playing to the moon.
The sound echoes in the faraway mountains.

"Take care and farewell!" the man says to Mirado.
"I can't do anything to help you now.
  But I can give you this flute."
  He puts his flute in Mirado's hand.
  The flute smells the same as Mirado's father's flute.

Once he gets over this mountain, the village of Paghman will not be far.
Encouraged, Mirado climbs the last peak.

Familiar mountains appear beyond the peak.

Mirado looks at the bottom of the valley and sees
the village he has longed for. He is almost in Paghman.
The wind blows through the valley and gently strokes Mirado's cheeks.
Slowly he starts down the path to the village.

The village is in ruins. It looks totally different.
"Hey, it's me, Mirado. I'm home!"

"What has happened to Yamo?"

Mirado walks from one end of the village to the other.

At the edge of the village stands a burnt plum tree.
It is the tree that Yamo and Mirado used to climb
together. Mirado looks at it carefully.
There are small buds at the tips of
the branches.

After a long winter, spring has
come to the village.

Mirado buries his father's flute under the plum tree.
Then he takes out the new flute and slowly starts playing.

♫ *DARA BA DARA*

*From valley to valley,*

*I will send a wind from Paghman to you.*

*A wind from my village, the most beautiful village in the world.* ♫

Early the next morning, while it is still dark, Mirado heads into town.

"I should be able to find Yamo there," he thinks.

Soon the town appears, rising out of a sea of mist.

In the morning sunlight, Mirado walks into the town.

The town is full of people.
Wonderful, familiar smells are everywhere.
But Mirado finds no one he knows.

He starts playing his flute on the street.

People gather around him.

He sees the ears of a donkey among the crowd.

♫ *The bright red beads, the cherries.*
   *Got them? Ate them? Or died without eating them?* ♫

Mirado hears a familiar voice singing.

He looks in the direction of the voice.

"Yamo!"

Yamo smiles at him.

"Welcome back, Mirado!"

In the same way they did on the day they said good-bye,
they hug each other tightly, touching cheek to cheek.

They will return to their village, carrying the bag of seeds.
Soon the village will be filled with green.

*The most beautiful village in the world is still waiting for everyone's return.*

**Yutaka Kobayashi** (1946–) is a Nihonga (Japanese-style paintings) artist and picture-book author. In 1979, his very first submission was accepted for the Japan Fine Arts Exhibition (Nitten), and in 1983 he received a Special Excellence Award in the Ueno Royal Museum Grand Prize Exhibition. He is a frequent visitor to the Islamic countries of Asia and the Middle East from 1970s to early 1980s, and the main themes of his works reflect from those visits.

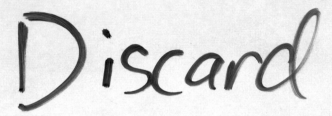

Return to the Most Beautiful Village in the World

Sekaiichi Utsukushii Murae Kaeru © 2003 Yutaka Kobayashi
All rights reserved.

Published in the United States / Canada by:
Museyon Inc.
333 East 45th Street
New York, NY 10017

Museyon is a registered trademark.
Visit us online at www.museyon.com

Originally published in Japan in 2003 by POPLAR Publishing Co., Ltd.
English translation rights arranged with POPLAR Publishing Co., Ltd.

Printed in China

ISBN 978-1-940842-45-5